My Mother's Voice

Quinn — all the best! *[signature]* 2008

By Joanne Ryder

Illustrated by Peter Catalanotto

HarperCollins*Publishers*

To my mother,
Dorothy McGaffney Ryder,
with love always

—J.R.

To my mom,
with love and admiration

—P.C.

As morning
begins,
my mother
calls me
from darkness
to light.

Her voice
is the sun
lighting
my day,
ever changing
with her
feelings,
yet ever
the same.

I follow
her laughter
from room
to room,
drawn to
her happiness.

I wrap her words
around me,
warm with
good wishes
for the day
to come.
"Have fun,"
she says.
"I hope you
do well."

And later,
when we meet,
her voice
is full of care,
asking
questions
till I
share
my day
with her.

Sometimes
her voice
is loud and clear.
I hear it
rising above
all others,
cheering me on.

Sometimes
I barely
hear her,
humming
as she works,
cheerful
as a robin
at sunup.

But when
she sings
a song
I know,
our voices
rise and fall
together,
mixing
into one.

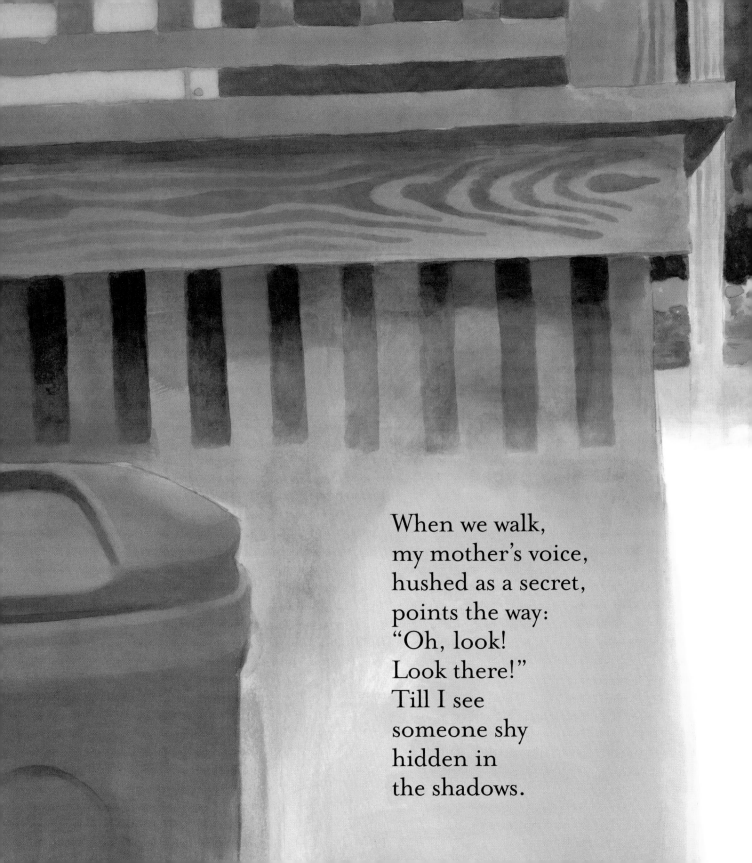

When we walk,
my mother's voice,
hushed as a secret,
points the way:
"Oh, look!
Look there!"
Till I see
someone shy
hidden in
the shadows.

And when
I'm sick or sad,
she wraps me
in her arms,
guards me
with her words:
"It will be okay, dear.
It will be okay."

There are times
my mother is quiet,
full of feelings
I cannot know.
So I wait,
quiet too,
wishing *her*
to be okay.

And soon
she strokes
my which-way hair,
drawing me
close to her
with words
she tickle-whispers
in my ear,
"I love you, dear."

At dusk,
I hear
my mother,
her voice
searching for me
through the grayness,
finding me,
and guiding me
home.

And when
I slip inside,
she smiles,
her voice
enfolding me
with just
one word.

No one
will ever
welcome me
and say it
quite the same—
my name.

My Mother's Voice • Text copyright © 2006 by Joanne Ryder • Illustrations copyright © 2006 by Peter Catalanotto • Manufactured in China. • All rights reser
No part of this book may be used or reproduced in any manner whatsoever without written permission except in the case of brief quotations embodied in cri
articles and reviews. For information address HarperCollins Children's Books, a division of HarperCollins Publishers, 1350 Avenue of the Americas, New Y
NY 10019. • www.harperchildrens.com • Library of Congress Cataloging-in-Publication Data • Ryder, Joanne. • My mother's voice / by Joanne Ryder ; illustr
by Peter Catalanotto.— 1st ed. • p. cm. • Summary: Lyrical text describes a mother's voice as she sings, hums, encourages, cheers, comforts, and shares secrets
her daughter during the course of a day. ISBN 0-06-029509-0 — ISBN 0-06-029510-4 (lib. bdg.) • [1. Voice—Fiction. 2. Mothers and daughters—Fict
3. Day—Fiction.] I. Catalanotto, Peter, ill. II. Title. • PZ7.R9752Myag 2006 2004030393 • [E]—dc22 • Designed by Stephanie Bart-Horvath •
1 2 3 4 5 6 7 8 9 10 • ❖ • First Edition